Where Did  They Go?

By Katrina-Jane

Hand Painted Artwork by: Allison Warry

SHANTI PUBLISHING

Shanti Publishing

Where Did They Go?

Helping Children Understand A Loved One's Passing

2ⁿᵈ Edition

Copyright © 2016 by Katrina-Jane

Printed in the United States of America

First Printing, 2016

ISBN: 978-0-9973754-5-9

Shanti Publishing

www.ShantiPublishing.com

All Images are the Hand Painted Artwork of: Allison Warry

Prologue

Dearest Parent/Guardian,

When a child loses someone they love, whether a relative, friend, or pet it is incredibly difficult for us to put into words what has happened in a way that they understand.

wrote this book for a very special 4-year-old named Archie and his 2-year-old sister Stella who didn't understand what was happening to their very much loved daddy, Alex who passed away.

I sincerely hope that this book helps you all in your time of grieving.

Love,

Katrina-Jane

Dedication

This book is dedicated to Archie and Stella, two amazingly brave and beautiful children.

I hope that this helps you understand where your daddy Alex has gone and that he will always be with you no matter where you go in life.

What happened to my
_____?
(insert name/title here)
Why did they die?
Grown-ups say they're in heaven
up there in the sky.

But if they are in the sky
And I catch a plane
Does that mean some day,
That I'll see them again?

O, my darling one
My precious little child
Come sit in my lap
And have a cuddle for awhile

Let me explain to you
At least I will try
Why you won't see them
When you're up in the sky

There are two parts to people
That's everyone you see
We each have a body
Just like you and like me

But there's a very special part of us
It's something you can't see
It's called our soul and it's special
And when we die it's set free.

So when our body's time
On this earth is done
Our soul goes to a special place
And it's way past the sun.

Some call it heaven
To describe where the soul goes
What it's really like,
Well, no-one really knows

We like to think of it
As a very special place
Where family, friends and pets go
All to live and play in heaven up in space

The soul says goodbye
To its body you see
It's time for it to go
It's time for it to be set free

Now, remember a soul
Isn't something you see
It's kind of like the wind
That blows through the trees

It's called a soul
That it's there but it's free
Sometimes it's called a spirit
That's when it visits you and me

Sometimes you may see
Their spirit when they are around
Or sometimes, they'll leave little messages
Like feathers on the ground

If you do see their spirit
You know not to be scared
They'll look just like you remember
And they've come back because they care

When their soul isn't here
They are up in heaven past the sun
But they can see what you're doing
They watch you play and having fun

They aren't sad
They want you to know
That they'll always be with you
And they will be watching you grow

So, all you need to remember
Each and every single day
That even though you can't see them
Their love will never go away

Now, my darling child
My precious little one
I hope this helps you understand
Where they have gone

The End...

About the Author

Katrina-Jane is a clairvoyant medium based in Newcastle NSW Australia.

Through working as a medium she deals with the passing of loved ones on a daily basis.

Parents have come to her asking for advice on how to explain this to their young children, whether the passing was a parent, grand-parent, friend or pet.

This book was inspired by two such children and she hopes that parents around the world will use it to help their little ones to understand what happens to us when we die.

Made in the USA
Coppell, TX
27 October 2023

23484320R00017